Space Explorers

Written by
Cath Jones

Illustrated by
Letizia Rizzo

Chapter 1

Yael rushed into the classroom. "Rob," she yelled. "Look at my new t-shirt!" She twirled on the spot and smiled happily.

"The Old Observatory," read Rob.

"We went there in the holidays," grinned Yael. "There was an *enormous* telescope and I looked at *space!* You know, planets and stars and stuff. And when you turn off the lights, my t-shirt glows in the dark!"

"Yael, quietly please!" interrupted her teacher, Ms French. "You'll be disturbing astronauts and aliens."

"Sorry!" laughed Yael.

Ms French called the class together. "This term's theme is *Explorers in Space*," she explained. "Your project work can be anything to do with this subject."

A dreamy look came into Yael's eyes. "Imagine being an astronaut exploring space! What an awesome job that would be."

Rob nodded. "But of course *you* couldn't be an astronaut."

"Why not?" Yael demanded.

"Well *obviously* girls can't be astronauts," said Rob.

Before Yael could reply, Ms French started to speak. "I have some news about an exciting space competition! Mrs Cobb will reveal the details in assembly. Line up please."

As they filed into the hall, Yael spotted a picture of a spaceship on the big screen. She muttered to Rob, "I bet girls *can* be astronauts."

Mrs Cobb, the headteacher, beamed at the pupils. "In a few minutes, we'll watch a live broadcast from the headquarters of the Space Alliance. They're about to announce a very special competition."

Right on cue, a smartly dressed woman appeared on the screen. Dr Jane was the director of the Space Alliance. For the next few minutes, Yael listened intently. The competition didn't sound *too* difficult. They had to come up with an experiment that could be carried out in zero gravity. The winners would visit the headquarters of the Space Alliance and be involved in a 'very exciting, once in a lifetime experience'.

Yael's head almost spun with excitement. "Rob!" she whispered. "Do you think the prize will be a trip into space? To the International Space Station?"

Rob looked doubtful. "I think that might be a bit dangerous."

Yael tugged on his sleeve. "*And* the director of the Space Alliance is a woman!" she said.

"I know. We just saw her. So?"

A triumphant look came onto Yael's face. "I bet she was an astronaut *before* she was the boss..."

"Maybe," he said.

"I'm sure girls *can* be astronauts. I'm going to prove it!" Yael said.

Chapter 2

Yael's class lined up outside the public library. The doors opened and Yael raced inside. She skidded to a halt in front of a bookcase and punched the air in triumph. She'd reached the space books before anyone else.

After a few moments, Rob appeared. "You could've waited for me," he moaned.

Behind him, Ms French rolled her eyes in despair. "No running!" she mouthed at Yael.

"Sorry!" said Yael. She grabbed a large hardback book from the shelf and waved it in front of Rob. "Look!"

He stared with a puzzled expression.

"*Women in Space!*" Yael whispered in delight. "You said girls can't be astronauts. I knew you couldn't be right!"

"Oh," said Rob in surprise. "Can I see?"

They settled down together on the floor cushions and turned the pages of the book.

"Valentina Tereshkova," Rob read.

"The first woman in space!" said Yael happily.

"But she wasn't an astronaut."

"Of course she was."

"Nope. It says here she was a *cosmo*naut. Not an *astro*naut."

"That's just because she was Russian! That's what they call their astronauts." Yael quickly flicked through the book. She jabbed her finger at a photograph of two women. "Look! In 2020, two women astronauts did a space walk together. Just them."

Yael jumped up and bleeped her library card on the self-service machine. "I'm going to borrow this. Do you want to do this term's project together?"

"On what exactly?" Rob asked.

"Women in space of course! I'll do all the research. And the writing… you could do the pictures. You're brilliant at drawing."

"Deal!" said Rob.

"And if we're going to win that Space Alliance competition, we'd better borrow lots of space books," said Yael.

"Win?!" exclaimed Rob. "Do you think we could?"

A serious look came into Yael's eyes. "Somebody

has to win so why not us?" She handed him a stack of books. "You have a look through these tonight, and tomorrow we can see what ideas we've come up with."

"I wonder what the prize is?" Rob said.

Yael leant forward and whispered, "I'm sure it's going to be something amazing!"

That night, Yael curled up in bed with the library books spread out around her. She turned the pages and studied the pictures. Above her, a tiny spider spun a web on the ceiling. She yawned. As sleep slipped over her, she wondered what it would feel like to blast into space.

Chapter 3

Ms French handed out science books. "You've got thirty minutes to come up with ideas for experiments that astronauts could carry out on the International Space Station. Let your imaginations run free..."

Yael grabbed a book and threw it open. She could hardly wait to get started.

"There's a whole chapter on experiments in space in this one," she said to Rob in an urgent whisper. "We've got to come up with something really good if we're going to win."

"I bet there'll be thousands of people entering the competition." Rob switched on his tablet and typed in 'experiments in space'. "You always take everything so seriously, Yael!"

Yael chewed the end of her pencil with a determined expression.

"I've already got some ideas," Rob said. "What about sending a cat and a mouse into space to see if they chase each other?

Yael laughed. "That would be funny but I'm not sure..."

"Or getting the astronauts to have a bubble bath," he continued, "and seeing what happens to the bubbles?"

She grinned. She didn't think they had a bath on the International Space Station!

For the next quarter of an hour, they searched for experiment ideas. Doubts began to fill Yael's mind. What if they couldn't come up with a winning idea?

Suddenly, Ms French clapped her hands. "Time's almost up!" she announced. "In a few minutes, we'll be watching a spaceship docking with the International Space Station *live*."

"We've got to hurry!" urged Yael.

Rob shook his head. "I can't think of anything else. What about you?"

For a moment, Yael hesitated. "Last night, just before I fell asleep, I spotted a spider dangling from my bedroom ceiling."

Rob shivered. "I don't like spiders."

"It was only a teeny weeny spider!"

"Okay, so what?"

"It was weaving a web."

Rob looked mystified. "And?"

"I wondered if a spider could do that in space? You know, weave a web in zero gravity?"

"Brilliant!" said Rob.

Yael turned a page in one of the science books. "It says here that dogs and monkeys have been sent into space."

"Two minutes left," interrupted Ms French.

"Quick! Write down the spider idea," Rob urged.

'Can Spiders Spin in Zero Gravity?' Yael wrote. She handed it in just as Ms French called time.

Rob gave Yael the thumbs up. "Well done," he whispered.

A few minutes later, as they watched the spaceship approaching the International Space Station, a wave

of excitement washed over Yael. Could her idea be a winner? Might she and Rob be blasted into space?

She gazed at the spaceship on the screen and stared at one of the astronauts. "Rob, look!" she gasped. She leant forward and peered closely. "That's a woman," she whispered. "I think *three* of the astronauts are women!"

Chapter 4

A few weeks later, Mrs Cobb called a special, whole school assembly. Yael gazed curiously around the hall. There was a picture of the International Space Station displayed on the screen. Butterflies of hope fluttered in her stomach. "Mrs Cobb looks very excited," she said.

"It must be about the competition!" Rob whispered back.

"The director of the Space Alliance has been in touch," announced Mrs Cobb. "She's studied all the experiment ideas, from all over the country." She paused and looked round the hall. "And I can now reveal the details of one of the winning experiments."

Yael crossed her fingers and closed her eyes.

"Two of the ten national winners are from this school," she continued.

Gasps of excitement filled the hall. Yael's eyes flew open. Her gaze met Rob's.

"The winners are in Ms French's class…"

Yael squeaked with excitement.

"The winning experiment…" announced Mrs Cobb in a loud voice, "is…"

Yael held her breath.

"'Can Spiders Spin in Zero Gravity?'!"

Rob let out a loud whoop. For a moment, Yael sat totally motionless, too dazed to move. Then she leapt to her feet and flung her arms into the air.

A few weeks later, a Space Alliance minibus arrived at school. Photographers from the local paper took pictures as Yael and Rob climbed aboard. *This feels like being a famous celebrity*, thought Yael. She waved happily at the other competition winners seated on the bus.

The journey to the Space Alliance headquarters seemed to fly by. By the time they arrived, Yael still had no idea what they had actually won. Nobody seemed to know anything. It was all very mysterious!

Yael gazed up at a modern, metal building.

"Welcome!" said a voice. It was Dr Jane, the director! "Please follow me."

She guided them into the building. "I expect you would like some refreshments," she continued. "I will reveal what your prize is a little later. I don't want to spoil the surprise! I promise it will be unforgettable!"

A long table was laid out with drinks and snacks. Smiling people milled around. Yael gazed around in wonder.

"This must be the staff canteen." She pointed at a row of framed photographs hanging the length of the room. "Those are all astronauts!"

Suddenly, Yael gasped. She stared at a woman walking towards them. "I'm sure she was in that 'Women in Space' book. She's been on the International Space Station!"

Rob gaped in astonishment.

"Jessica! The astronaut!" Yael called.

The woman strode towards them. She high-fived Yael. "Congratulations on winning the competition. I'm looking forward to your experiment."

Yael felt like she could float with happiness.

Rob gulped nervously and shook hands with the astronaut. "Please could I take a photograph for our space project?" he asked shyly.

"Sure thing! Selfie?" she asked as Rob handed her his phone.

Rob nodded.

"Smile!" The screen flashed and she handed back Rob's phone. Then she turned and strode away. "I'll catch you later," she called over her shoulder.

"Wow," murmured Rob.

"Awesome!" said Yael.

Chapter 5

A hush fell over the room as the director glanced down at her clipboard.

"This is it!" whispered Yael.

"The moment has come to reveal the details of your prize," said the director.

Yael's heart thumped in her chest. She was so excited she could hardly breathe! Beside her, Rob's eyes were like saucers.

"I must apologise for the secrecy," continued the director. "It must have appeared rather mysterious!"

Yael nodded in silent agreement.

"Today you will have the opportunity to be part of something top secret! In a few moments, you will be issued with special suits."

"I bet they're spacesuits!" gasped Yael. "We *are* going to be blasted into space!"

Rob began to sweat. "I'm not sure I want to go into space," he mumbled.

The director smiled reassuringly. "I think some of you are hoping that you are going to become astronauts!" She laughed. "You'll have to wait until you are a little older for that!"

A look of relief flashed across Rob's face. But Yael was swamped with disappointment. She *wasn't* going into space...

"Today we are inviting you to travel on our top secret, zero gravity jet; you will be passengers on a parabolic flight!"

Yael's face brightened. A zero gravity jet flight sounded pretty awesome.

"Parabolic flight?" Rob repeated in a puzzled voice.

"Let me explain." The director pointed through the window at a shiny, silver jet parked on the runway. "Our jet will take off and then carry out a series of large arcs in the sky. This is called parabolic flight."

"Awesome!" murmured Yael.

"Each arc will allow you to experience the feeling of weightlessness. Exactly like an astronaut in space, you will be able to float or fly like a superhero!"

For a few moments, the room was silent as the news sank in. Then all the children began to chatter excitedly.

The director raised her voice. "This is your astronaut crew who will be looking after you from now on. Please follow Helen, Kate, Jessica, Bob and Chris. They'll help you put on your jumpsuits and assist you during the flight."

Jessica led the children into a room full of jumpsuits. Each one had a label with a name on it. "The adults responsible for you sent us your sizes. They have signed all the relevant consent forms for your flight too!"

"Awesome!" said Yael as she pulled on her jumpsuit. It fitted perfectly.

"I don't know how you managed to get in so easily," Rob muttered. "I'm so hot. It's really uncomfortable!"

Helen took photographs of the children in their jumpsuits. "If anyone doesn't wish to proceed with the flight, they can of course withdraw at any moment. Just come and have a chat with one of us," she said.

Rob gazed at Yael. "I'm scared of flying."

"You don't have to go," she said.

He hesitated, unsure what to do.

She squeezed his hand. "I'll look after you if you do come. We're a team!"

There was a bus waiting on the runway to take them to the jet. Rob took a deep breath and followed Yael.

Chapter 6

Yael stared out of the window as the bus sped across the runway. The sleek, silver jet glittered in the bright sunshine. "Is this really happening?" she whispered to Rob. "It feels like a dream!"

He stamped his boots on the floor with a loud thud. "That doesn't sound like a dream!"

The astronauts led the way up the steps onto the jet. Yael found it hard not to giggle. It was just too exciting now they were there!

"Welcome on board our parabolic lab!" said Kate.

"Here on the jet, we have created a flying laboratory where gravity-free experiments can be carried out without the need to travel into space."

"As soon as you've taken a seat and buckled up, we'll take off," added Chris.

Yael made sure she was sitting next to Rob. The jet engines revved and she felt the whole jet vibrating. They stared out of the window and hung on tightly to their seat belts as the aeroplane raced along the runway. All the children whooped and cheered when the jet roared into the air.

Within a few minutes, the astronauts had unbuckled their seatbelts. They divided themselves between the children.

"Hello again," said Jessica to Yael and Rob. "I'm *your* helper. Follow me please."

The jet was much larger than Yael had expected. They soon found themselves in an open area like a large room.

"This is where we'll spend most of the flight," explained Jessica. "Each parabolic arc the jet flies will give us approximately twenty to thirty seconds of zero gravity. You'll feel lighter than a feather!"

Yael almost trembled with excitement.

"Everyone please lie down on the floor," instructed Chris.

Rob let out a loud sigh. "I can't believe the things you get me into!"

Yael squeezed his hand.

"There's no need for special equipment," said Jessica. "Give a little push and you'll find yourself floating up to the ceiling!

The jet began to climb. Suddenly, Yael felt a change. She couldn't help laughing as she began to float away from the floor!

"Watch what happens," said Jessica as she squirted a water bottle at Rob. The water formed into balls and floated away.

Yael turned an effortless somersault

and Rob ran up the wall and sat on the ceiling.

Before the jet began its second arc, Jessica handed

a large box to Yael and Rob. "You'll find everything

you need to carry out your experiment."

There were two spiders in the box sitting in a web.

As Yael felt herself float off the floor, both the spiders

began to float too. The spiders were adding threads

to their web but, whenever they let go, rather than dropping to the bottom of the box, they floated! Yael and Rob high fived.

Their experiment had worked. Spiders *could* spin webs in zero gravity!

Chapter 7

As the children walked out of the headquarters of the Space Alliance, Yael felt like she was still floating. She nudged Rob and grinned at him.

"Thanks," he said.

"What for?"

"For everything. You believed we could win. The experiment was your idea and..." his voice trailed off.

Yael looked at him questioningly. "What?"

"Thanks for looking after me."

Yael smiled and shrugged. "That's just what friends do."

The minibus was waiting to take the children home. As they stepped on board, the director handed them each a shiny, silver bag. When it was Yael's turn, the director shook Yael's hand and smiled. "Perhaps one day you will come and work here," she said. "I'm sure you would make a fine astronaut."

Yael beamed. For once, she was speechless. The director thought she would make a good astronaut!

Everyone waved and shouted goodbye and thanks as they pulled away.

Rob rustled his bag. "I wonder what they've given us."

Yael peered in. Her face lit up as she pulled out a framed photograph of herself in the jumpsuit.

Rob leant over and examined the picture. He grinned. "You look like a proper astronaut!"

Yael raised her eyebrows. "What, even though I'm a girl?"

Rob looked a bit sheepish and laughed. "You're good at maths and science and super sporty and really brave! I reckon you'd make a brilliant astronaut!"

Silence settled over the minibus; the children were lost in thought.

Yael closed her eyes. She almost glowed with happiness. The director had said the prize was a once in a lifetime experience. But if one day she did become an astronaut, zero gravity would be normal!

Spider Space Facts!

Back in **1973**, astronauts took Arabella and Anita, two European garden spiders, into space to see if they could spin webs in zero gravity and they could!

In **2011**, Gladys and Esmeralda, golden orb-weaver spiders, joined astronauts on the International Space Station.

You can find out more information about the spiders by visiting NASA's website.

Discussion Points

1. What did Yael take home from the Old Observatory in the holidays?

2. Who doesn't think women can be astronauts to begin with?

a) Rob

b) Yael

c) Ms French

3. What was your favourite part of the story?

4. How did the aeroplane create a sense of zero gravity for everyone on board?

5. Do you think it is tricky to walk in a spacesuit? Why?

6. Who was your favourite character and why?

7. There were moments in the story when Yael had to face **prejudice**. Where do you think the story shows this most?

8. What do you think happens after the end of the story?

Book Bands for Guided Reading

The Institute of Education book banding system is a scale of colours that reflects the various levels of reading difficulty. The bands are assigned by taking into account the content, the language style, the layout and phonics. Word, phrase and sentence level work is also taken into consideration.

The Maverick Readers Scheme is a bright, attractive range of books covering the pink to grey bands. All of these books have been book banded for guided reading to the industry standard and edited by a leading educational consultant.

To view the whole Maverick Readers scheme, visit our website at

www.maverickearlyreaders.com

Or scan the QR code to view our scheme instantly!

Maverick Chapter Readers
(From Lime to Grey Band)